LEO'S ANGEL

DARREN EDWARDS

CONTENTS

Leo's Angel is a work of fiction. Names, characters, places, and incidents are the products of the author's imagination or are used fictitiously. Any resemblance to actual events, locales, or persons, living or dead, is entirely coincidental.

Printed in the United States of America

ISBN: 979-8-218-30052-4
LCCN: 2023919901

To My Son Luca

PROLOGUE

It was Thanksgiving day but all that was on our table was brillo pads and ashtrays. I was twelve years old and an only child. My mother and father had run out of crack to smoke, and although they were crack addicts they were still very much in love. My father had a special kind of love for my mother. A love that I had never seen before. He never stopped opening car doors for her. On birthdays and anniversaries, he would always bring her flowers. Sometimes he brought them unexpectedly. Those were the ones that put the biggest smile on her face.

Our kitchen was the same size as our living room and I could stand in both at the same time. It wasn't much but it was all we needed. I sat on the counter near the kitchen window watching cars go by. My mother sat at the table smoking a kool one hundred while my father looked shamelessly all over the floor for any pieces of crack that may have fallen. The days of them trying to hide anything from me were long gone. I wasn't even a teenager yet but I was very aware of everything that went on around me.

They started off hosting house parties where they and some of their friends would play dominoes and card games. During the parties they tried to make me go to bed, but how could anyone expect a child to sleep with music blasting through the speakers while people laughed and talked loudly. Sooner or later they stopped caring about me going to bed and let me stay up with them as they smoked weed and drank forties. I still remember the first time I saw my dad snort a line of cocaine off of the table. One drug led to another and now they were full blown crack addicts.

"Linda, call Joe and see where he's at."

"Calm down Percy, I just talked to him ten minutes ago, he'll be here soon enough."

Joe was the neighborhood drug dealer. He was an Italian guy in his thirties who had moved down south from New Jersey. He always wore the nicest clothes and drove the best cars. Everybody loved Joe, including me. He had a certain charisma about him that attracted people, and I wanted to be just like him. When I saw Joe's car turn into the driveway, I was glad because now my father could get up off the floor and act like a normal person. I ran out the door to greet him and walked up to his all white 1985 Cutlass as he was getting out of it. His hair was slicked back. He wore black jeans all the way up on his waist with a white t-shirt tucked in. He always wore a black leather jacket that stopped right at his waist and fit him nice and snug.

"Wassup Joe?"

"Wassup lil man, Happy Thanksgiving!"

He handed me a grocery bag with three to-go plates inside of it before discreetly slipping me a ten dollar bill.

"Here, put this in your pocket before your parents see."

Joe always gave me money. He always looked out for everybody in the neighborhood. He always said, "If you look out for people, chances are they'll look out for you as well."

He rubbed the top of my head before heading toward our front door. I stayed outside to admire his car. I also didn't wanna hear my mother's mouth about being in *grown folks' business.*

1

LEO

I had just gotten off the phone with my father. He was in jail awaiting trial for murder. Not just any murder, but the murder of my mother. My father would have never laid a hand on my mother. I knew in my heart he was innocent, but knowing wasn't enough. The problem was I couldn't prove it. Ever since my mother was strangled to death almost five years ago, my main focus in life was to find her real killer. This way my father could be set free and the person responsible could go to prison. That is if I didn't kill him first. Needless to say, I haven't been that successful in my search. For a while, I searched through all the repeat offenders in my neighborhood. The ones who were back and forth to jail for trespassing, public intoxication, assault and battery, and other miscellaneous petty crimes. I even went as far as to kidnap a guy named Jimmy Johnson, who was the most suspicious person on my list. His arrest record was much longer than anyone else's. He even made repeat offender of the month in the Jail Report with close to two dozen mugshots. I blindfolded him, tied him up, took him to a disclosed location, and tried to beat a confession out of him. He cried and denied having anything to do with it until I realized that I was probably making a big mistake.

"Say hello to my little friend!" I watched Scarface as I sat on my couch smoking a blunt. I was a neat freak so other than the weed smoke that filled the air, my crib was immaculate. I knew organization was the key to success, and success was exactly what I was after. Scarface was a Cuban pushing forty and I was a twenty-two-year-old Black man. Even in our differences, we had some similarities. We both came from little to nothing and were trying to beat the odds against us. We both sold cocaine with dreams of taking over the world. It seemed like I was well on my way since I hadn't been to jail in two years. It may not seem like a big achievement, but it was my longest run yet since I started getting into trouble as a juvenile. Like so many others, jail was like a revolving door.

It was obvious they weren't going to let my father out, and with his trial date inching closer I had to find my mother's killer. I couldn't do that from behind bars so I had to stay focused, especially since the judge said he wasn't going to keep playing with me. I'm pretty sure his exact words were, "If I see you in my courtroom again Mr. Bryant, you're gonna regret it."

I wasn't quite making moves like Scarface but maybe in due time. I was currently renting a mobile home and had about twenty thousand dollars to my name. It was pennies to some people, but it was actually pretty decent compared to most of the so-called hustlers in Augusta,

Georgia. I wasn't like them. I wasn't like anybody. I was very introverted and hung by myself, but I knew the city like the back of my hand. As I got older Joe taught me a lot, mostly about the dope game. He always kept me straight with whatever I needed whenever I needed it. When I wasn't moving around the city making plays I was at home. I watched movies like Scarface, Paid In Full, and New Jack City, though I always turned to Seinfeld when it came on. That was my favorite show.

A stream of sunlight shined through the edge of my window in between the curtain and the wall. It was a peaceful morning like most of my days. I thought about what I would do later. My mind juggled getting another tattoo, and taking my dogs to the park so they could run around and play. I ashed my blunt in a large coffee can that badly needed to be dumped. A group of shadows glided quickly across my wall and made me sit up wondering why so many people were so close to my trailer.

Boom! Boom! Boom! Three loud bangs hit my front door, and my heart skipped two beats.

"Richmond County Sheriff's Department! Open the door now!"

2

ANGEL

Lately, I had been dolling myself up with makeup and clothes that made me feel more attractive. My golden brown skin matched my brown earth-tone hair. My light pink sundress didn't fail to compliment my almost perfect backside. Feeling extra sexy, I leaned on the handle of the grocery cart as I made my way down the chip aisle. With so many options of chips to choose from you would think it would be harder to decide on which ones to get. For me, it was a no brainer. I grabbed a family-sized bag of nacho cheese Doritos and threw them into my cart on top of the sliced turkey. I had to do the grocery shopping for myself. I finally didn't have to think about anybody's preferences before grabbing what I wanted.

"I love you too Daddy. See y'all tomorrow."

I hung up the phone after making plans to go eat dinner with my family. I knew they missed me. I had only seen them a handful of times since I moved out almost a year ago.

I was the outcast of the family or as my mom would say *the ghetto girl*. I was twenty-one years old and living on my own. They always checked on me to make sure I was okay, especially lately. I needed it though because of how lost and confused I had been feeling. Sometimes I didn't know whether I was coming or going so hearing their voices always made me feel better.

My little brother Fletcher was nine years old. My parents had him when I was twelve, not too long after I found out how babies were made. Around that time all I could think about was my parents doing the nasty. After being the only child for so long I had to get used to not having all the attention on me anymore. I used to babysit him when both my parents had to work, and at times it seemed like I was the one that gave birth to him. I knew he was happy I would be visiting tomorrow.

I finished shopping, paid for my groceries, and headed toward my jeep. I planned to go home and put my groceries up, then head to the mall for a mani and pedi. Once in the parking lot, my stomach sounded off like two lions fighting. I was definitely going to stop by Charley's Grilled Subs when I got to the mall. In the meantime, I ripped open a box of Slim Jims.

3

LEO

The police banged on the door so loud that my two rottweilers Billy and Jean were in my backyard going crazy. I started breathing deeply as lines formed between my forehead. Questions arose in my head that I had no time to answer. The only thing I was thinking was that I couldn't go back to jail, not here, not now. They banged on the door again.

"Last chance, open the door now!"

I had to think quickly. I grabbed my money, pistol, weed, and cocaine and shoved it into my backpack as fast as I could. I slung my backpack over my shoulders and pulled both of the straps as tight as they could get. I bolted toward my backdoor and lunged through it. To no surprise, officers were waiting on the side of my trailer with their guns drawn.

"Put your hands up and get on the ground!"

That never stopped me before and it wasn't about to stop me now. I ran past my dogs headed toward what seemed to be the tallest fence in the world. It was roughly ten feet tall and separated my backyard from a large wooded area. The voices of the officers clashed with the sound of my barking dogs.

On the other side of the fence, I hit the ground and took off running as fast as I could. I got about fifteen or twenty feet before the sound of two gunshots immediately followed by the gut wrenching howls of Billy and Jean stopped me dead in my tracks. My body froze and I stood up straight. Not my babies. Pain and sadness tried to take over, but I had to keep running. While I ran for my life, I dodged trees and low hanging branches. The woods seemed never ending. I ran for what felt like an eternity. Other than the thought of getting away my mind was empty. There was no room left for anything else. The gap between me and the officers continued to grow. I had gotten a substantial lead on them but I didn't slow up. In fact, I did the opposite and turned it up a notch. I dug deep down inside of myself and found the energy to make myself run faster. Thank God I had on my Air Maxes and not my slides like I usually wore around the house.

The filthy backside of the upcoming shopping center looked promising as I approached it. For a second, I thought about jumping in one of the three garbage dumpsters lined up against the back of the building. But surely just like in the movies that would be the first place they look. I had no idea how I was gonna get away. What I did know was that my father needed me and my mother needed real justice. I couldn't go back to jail. I was ready to do whatever it took.

4

LEO

My feet started to drag the ground as I struggled to catch my breath. I wiped my face in an attempt to keep the sweat out of my eyes. I raced through the breezeway only to slow up before reaching the parking lot of the shopping center. I didn't need to draw any attention to myself. Rent A Center, Citi Trends, and Mike's Sub Shop lined one side. On the opposite side was a Food Lion which was responsible for the majority of the cars. I needed to get some wheels fast. I had to get outta dodge before the whole place was lit up with police lights.

There was a couple with what I guessed to be their daughter walking into the Food Lion, and two old ladies coming out of the sub shop. I needed an easy target, somebody who was alone so I could borrow their car and get as far away as possible. I was running out of time. Just as I was about to take off running again I noticed a thick, curvy, brown skinned chick in a pink sundress returning her cart. Look at God. I knew it was my only chance. I had to make a move.

Just like the rest of the world, her head was stuck in her phone. She walked back to her black Jeep Patriot unaware of the life changing moment that was about to take place. As soon as she opened her door I crept up from behind. With my right hand, I forced my gun into her lower back and placed my left hand on her shoulder.

"Climb in the passenger seat now unless you wanna die today." I said, trying to sound as serious as possible without getting too loud.

"We all gotta die sometime," she said.

Not exactly the response I was going for. I wrapped my arm around her neck and pushed my gun harder into her lower back.

"Okay okay damn," she said.

She climbed over the driver seat and into the passenger. Her perfectly sized ass jiggled through her sundress and for a split second, I forgot what I was doing. As soon as she was in the passenger seat I jumped in as fast as I could. With the car already started, I put it in drive and pulled off. My gun was still pointed at her, though she didn't seem scared at all as I eased toward the closest shopping center exit. Glancing back in the rearview I saw about a half dozen officers standing at the end of the breezeway. Some with their hands on their hips looking around in confusion, others with their hands on their knees trying to catch their breath. From the looks of it, I had barely gotten away.

Pulling out of the parking lot, I took my gun off of her but kept it in my hand.

"Look, I'm not gonna hurt you."

She looked me in my eyes.

"Trust me, I'm not worried about that."

What the hell did I get myself into? Not only were the police after me but now I had a whole hostage. All I knew was that I wasn't stopping. Whether she liked it or not she was stuck with me. Getting onto the interstate, I headed toward Atlanta, Georgia.

"If you're not gonna hurt me then why are you still holding that gun, Mr. Badguy?"

I gave her a look that was plain and cold. Was she really tryna be funny at a time like this? Maybe she wanted an answer. Either way, I understood. I put the gun down out of her reach. As soon as I put the gun down she turned around to grab something from the backseat. I went to reach for the gun again before I saw she was holding a bag of Doritos. She opened them and threw one in her mouth as if she didn't have a care in the world.

"You're really not scared are you?" I asked, chuckling.

"If ima be held hostage, I might as well eat right?"

She scolded me as if I didn't feel bad enough already. She threw back a few more chips before holding the bag out in my direction. I couldn't believe she was offering me some of her food after I kidnapped her at gunpoint. I looked at her for a moment before reaching my hand in the bag. "Thanks."

"So why are you running from the police?" she asked. "You don't kill people do you?"

"Only people who ask too many questions," I said.

She rolled her eyes and sucked her teeth. "Oh, now I'm really scared."

"Listen, as soon as I get where I'm going you can have your car back and do as you please lil mama."

"And where exactly are you going?"

I thought about it for a second.

"I don't know yet."

"Perfect," she said as she laid her seat all the way back and looked out the window.

We rode down the interstate for a while in an awkward silence. The trees on the side of the road now seemed full of life. Every time somebody rode past us, I thought to myself how lucky they were to not be in my position. Then something dawned on me. "Gimme your phone."

"Excuse me."

"I said gimme your phone. Don't make me change my mind on what I said about not hurting you."

"Yea whatever, calm down Mr. Rambo."

She pulled her phone out of her bra and handed it to me. I powered it off and set it next to my gun out of her reach.

"So what's your name?" I asked.

"It might as well be Ms. hostage right now."

"So you think you're funny, huh? What's the name your parents gave you?"

She cut her eyes at me before answering.

"Angel."

"Oh shit, damn I guess you were my Angel today," I said as I looked back through the rearview mirror.

"So are you gonna tell me your name too, or do you just want me to call you Mr. Badguy?" I shook my head in amazement and then looked into her eyes.

"You just don't quit do you? My name is Leo."

5

LEO

The interstate in front of me looked like a long open road of questions. What was I gonna do? Where was my life heading? I couldn't go back to Augusta anytime soon because by now I'm sure the local news was covered with my face. It's difficult starting over but at this point, it was better than going backwards. I didn't wanna make any stops but the gas tank was on Ezekiel. I pulled into a small deserted gas station about an hour outside of Atlanta. I got out of the car, went around to her side, and opened her door.

"Walk in here with me real quick, and don't get any bright ideas."

"Damn, I shared my chips with you and you still don't trust me?"

While getting out of the car she balled up both her fist and jumped at me. I guess she was trying to make me flinch but it didn't work. This girl was something else, nothing like I'd ever seen before. I held the door for her as we walked into the empty gas station. It smelled like cleaning supplies and boiled peanuts. An elderly Asian man sat behind the counter with his eyes closed. He reminded me of the old man from *The Karate Kid*. He jumped up, opening his eyes when he heard the door shut behind us. His voice was shaky when he greeted us. Old slot machines lined the front wall and on the back wall were coolers. Only four aisles sat in the middle of the store. Other than him there wasn't a soul in sight.

"Can I get forty on pump one and five packs of Swisher Sweets?"

Angel stood right next to me with her arms crossed and her bottom lip poked out. She was still pouting about having to get out of the car. As I was grabbing my change from Sleepyhead the door to the store swung open behind me. I turned to see who it was and was greeted with a long barrel revolver. Isn't it crazy how karma works? I was just holding Angel at gunpoint, now I was the one in front of the gun. I didn't think the day could get any more interesting. The gunman was wearing a mask, gloves, and long sleeves, but I could tell he was white by the rim of his eyes.

"Get on the ground!" he said as he waved the revolver back and forth between me, Angel, and Sleepyhead who was now wide awake. "Not you old man! You put the money in the bag!"

I tried to position myself between Angel and his gun as we lowered to our knees. I looked back at her and once again she didn't look afraid. Was she used to getting guns drawn on her or something? I looked back at the masked man waiting on the perfect moment to pull out my gun and show this motherfucker he robbed the wrong store today. It didn't take long for Sleepyhead to put the money in the bag. By the looks of the place, it couldn't have been more than a couple hundred dollars. When he leaned over the counter to grab the bag of money, it was my opportunity. I had to, for all I knew he could kill all of us so he wouldn't leave any witnesses. I wasn't gonna give him the chance. Besides, I didn't take anybody pointing a gun at me lightly. I reached in my back pocket only to realize my gun wasn't there. Hearing a loud gunshot blast immediately made my ears ring. Everything froze for a moment. The robber dropped to the floor, and I looked over at Angel to see her pointing my gun in the direction of where he was standing. Her hands were shaking but her face was plain and cold. I grabbed the gun, put it in my pocket, and pulled her in for a hug. He wasn't moving and blood was starting to form a pool around his head. I was sure he was dead. That made it twice in one day that she had saved my life, and for that I was grateful. She really was my Angel.

"Come on, we gotta get outta here."

I grabbed her hand and pulled her behind me as we raced out of the store. "Thank you!" yelled the store clerk on our way out the door.

6

LEO

The rest of the ride to Atlanta was a quiet one, to say the least. There wasn't much to be said. What happened was in the past and we couldn't change it. I felt guilty but something was telling me to keep my thoughts to myself while we were still on the road.

We pulled into a two-story motel on the east side of Atlanta. It wasn't exactly the Ritz Carlton but we had to blend in. It looked like the maintenance man was on vacation from all the trash scattered throughout the parking lot. Junkies that could pass for zombies roamed around. A group of kids consisting of all different ethnicities were standing around in a circle talking. I glanced over at Angel who was looking straight ahead with no emotion. I noticed she wasn't blinking until I put my hand on her knee which seemed to bring her back to reality.

"Look, this is all my fault. You would've never had to shoot him if I never kidnapped you in the first place. I don't know whether to say thank you for saving my life, or sorry for getting you into this bullshit."

She looked at me and placed her hand on top of mine halfway interlocking our fingers.

"You don't have to say anything. I'm just glad we're okay."

"Yea, me too," I said.

She offered to go inside the lobby and check into the room for us. It wasn't hard to trust her now that she had killed somebody right in front of me. The Arabs that owned the place had us pay a little extra for her not having an I.D. The last thing I needed was to be tracked down by the police for us using our information.

Inside the room was nothing fancy. Besides the two beds, there was only a tv, dresser, table, and a mini-fridge.

"Look we gotta lay low for a while, at least until shit cools down," I said.

I let her shower first and then I took one myself. Afterward, I bust down a swisher sweet. It had been a long day and I was finally able to relax for a while and smoke. I turned on the TV and flipped through the channels before stopping on World's Wildest Police Chases.

"Hey, we might see you on there," she said.

I gave her a blank stare. "Real funny."

I passed her the blunt and she took a long hard pull. Normally I'd get mad at somebody for dragging my blunt like that, but she had been through a lot today. When the blunt got short I sat it in the motel ashtray and slid closer to her on the edge of the bed.

"I'm sorry again for getting you in this shit. I just want

you to know I got your back like you had mine. Anything you need I got you, I promise."

"Thanks," she said.

I opened my arms to hug her. The way she sunk into my chest I could tell she needed one. She smelled good. It was a mixture of the motel's lemon soap, cocoa butter lotion, and some spray she kept in her purse. The longer we hugged the tighter we held each other. I finally loosened my grip and rubbed the back of her neck. She jumped as her body let out a jolt of pleasure, and I felt my man man start to grow. Anytime man man got involved I was no longer the decision maker, he called all the shots.

There was no looking back now. I put my right hand firmly around her throat. She moaned and pulled back in a fake attempt to loosen from my grip. She fell back on the bed as I lept on top of her. Both her nose and forehead were touching mine.

"Gimme your tongue," I said.

She stuck her tongue out and I put my mouth around it and looked her in her eyes as I rubbed her through her panties. She was wetter than a pair of rainboots in a flood. I continued to suck her tongue as I put two fingers inside her. That made her go crazy. She was shaking and moaning. Now man man was at full attention. I had to have her. I had to have her now.

7

TONY

Me and my twin brother Travis sat in my black Impala just outside the brightness of the street light. *Trouble* by Lil Boosie played just loud enough that we could hear it without drawing any attention. I put an Applebee's gift card to my nose and took a good sized bump before handing Trav the card along with a folded twenty-dollar bill filled with coke. I lost count of how many ecstasy pills I had popped throughout the day, but if I had to guess the one I just swallowed was probably number six or seven. The automatic guns that sat in both of our laps weren't at all unfamiliar. The murders we did in Augusta were only the recent bodies we accumulated throughout our lives. Florida was like World War II compared to the little beefs we encountered here. Growing up in one of the most dangerous projects in Dade County we were swallowed up by the street life before we could make any decisions for ourselves. Going to war over territory, money, drugs, or even just respect had become a part of us that couldn't be removed. Tonight was just another day in the office.

"Man, where the hell is this motherfucker at? If he don't come out soon we shootin' the whole fuckin crib up," Travis said sitting in the passenger seat.

"Calm down bruh, he's gonna be dead soon enough, hell ain't got no closing time," I said.

True enough we looked exactly alike, but I definitely was the one with more sense. My brother was a loose cannon, ready to kill anything that got in his way without asking any questions. Sometimes I wondered if he was this way because of the shit we've been through or if he was just a lil bit slow in the head.

I knew Sambo was inside his house going about his night as usual, unaware he would be doing everything for the last time. In this thing we call the streets, running off with someone's drugs or money without attempting to contact them was a death certificate just waiting to be signed. Me and Travis didn't mind putting our John Handcock on em', no matter who it was. Nobody ran off with our money and lived to tell about it. Florida and Georgia were two different states but the same principles applied to us no matter where we were. When it came down to our money, nobody got a pass.

The porch light came on. I sat all the way up in my seat and grabbed my gun out of my lap. Trav was already clutching when I looked over. The door to the house swung open and Sambo came walking out. Trav climbed out of the window and sat on the door as his arms rested on the roof of the car. As Sambo went to walk down the steps, I put the car in drive and rolled slowly out of the darkness. He stopped halfway down the steps when he noticed my car. It was too late.

I let my gun spray out of my driver window as Trav shot over the top of the car. Fire from both guns lit up the night. I didn't have to hold my trigger long before all thirty rounds spit out quickly into Sambo, his house, and whoever was inside. He had no time to run or shoot back. His body fell to the bottom of the steps, lying still on the concrete sidewalk. He was dead. Not even Curtis Jackson could have survived that many bullets. I rode off slowly and made a right. I started the song over from the beginning and turned the volume up. Another kill, another dead body, but most importantly another example made. Nobody was gonna play with us.

8

LEO

I woke up the next morning next to Angel's naked body. The feeling was bittersweet. Not only was I on the run, but was now responsible for her being on the run too, though she seemed not to care as much. It kind of really didn't seem like that big of a deal after three long rounds of rough sweaty sex. With all the frustration I had built up, I needed it and I could tell she did too. I also needed to get some fresh air and clear my head. I definitely wasn't going to make anything happen sitting inside the room all day. I got out of bed slowly, trying not to wake her. Although I doubt anyone could get her out of that deep sleep the way she was snoring.

I sat on the walkway outside of the room and lit up a blunt. Looking down between the rails I saw a group of kids playing tag. The way they were vibing together it was obvious they weren't just staying the night. It was a motel but it felt more like the projects. The feel wasn't too different from Augusta. I noticed an all too familiar sound, it was an ice cream truck turning in. The truck was white with big blue stripes and had pictures of ice cream covering the side of the truck. When it came to a stop, an older Hispanic man leaned on his arms with his head peering out of the window. A younger guy with his shirt off and a lot of tattoos came out of nowhere and bought ice cream for all the kids. It reminded me of how Joe used to buy ice cream off the truck in my neighborhood when I was little. Joe had a lot to do with me becoming who I was, some of it good and some of it bad. Either way, I loved seeing shit like that. The bright smiles on those kid's faces were worth more than money.

I didn't know anybody in Atlanta. I didn't have any clientele. And although it felt similar to home, if I was gonna survive on the run I had to link with somebody and get some product off. I'm pretty sure I had the perfect idea of where to start.

The same guy that just put all of the kids on a sugar rush was strolling down the balcony towards me. From the way he walked, you would think he owned the place. He had the same dark complexion as me as well as the same physique, only he was about five inches shorter.

"Damn, dat smell like some gas my boy. What's up, my name June."

He extended his fist for a pound.

"Leo," I said as I bumped my fist into his. "I saw what you did for those kids over there."

"Yea, most of their parents are either strung out or prostitutes. I try to look out for 'em as much as I can, you feel me."

"That's wassup, I know they appreciate it, blessings are definitely gonna come back to you." "Well, if you sell me some of that gas, that'll be a blessing."

I followed him down the walkway to his room which was about six doors down from ours.

Inside his room had an at-home feel. It immediately reminded me of a dorm room. There was a calendar on the wall right next to the beds. On the opposite side of the room were two posters. One was a young Mariah Carey in jean shorts and an orange bikini top. The other poster was of a bright red 1964 Chevy Impala with twenty-inch spokes. Dishes were stacked neatly by the sink and the light by the bathroom was replaced with a neon bulb that changes colors every few seconds.

"Make yourself at home, my boy."

"Appreciate you fam, how much gas were you trying to get?"

"Lemme just get a vick."

I tossed him a quarter ounce of pink runtz. He held it to his nose and inhaled. "Yes sir! How much I owe you, my boy?"

"You good fam, I told you blessings were coming your way."

His head tilted to the side as he smiled.

"Besides, I might need your help. What you know about the cocaine business?" He smiled even harder this time, sitting all the way up in his chair.

"That's my thing right there, bruh. I serve a lil bit, and I know some cats that'll spend big if it's good. Why, you the plug?' he asked.

I looked him in his eyes.

"Nah, lil bruh I ain't the plug," I said. "We the plug."

9

ANGEL

When I woke up and looked around, Leo was gone. It all felt like one big dream. Though it wasn't a dream at all. It was my new reality. I killed a man yesterday, which didn't really phase me as much as I thought it would. I also had hot, sweaty, passionate sex with Leo last night. Sure I had sex before but nothing like that. He Knew how to boss up and take control of me. He handled me like I've needed to be handled for so long and I loved it. Not to mention he was tall, handsome, smart, and funny.

It dawned on me that I didn't call my parents and tell them I wasn't coming to dinner. How could I when he still had my phone hostage? I thought for a while about what lie I would tell them about why I couldn't make it. Either way, I knew my Dad would be upset. I got out of the bed and showered. After all that sweaty sex, the hot water felt so good. I leaned up against the shower wall and let it fall down on my head and chest. After I showered I cleaned the room then decided to fix sandwiches for me and Mr. Whodini, wherever he was. Good thing I went grocery shopping before I was kidnapped. I flipped through the channels and couldn't find anything good to watch so I left it on this show called Ridiculousness. It was a bunch of clips of people doing all types of crazy things.

A little while later the room door opened, and Mr. Whodini was doing his reappearing act. "Hey Zaddy," I said, smiling from ear to ear.

He laughed. "Wassup bae."

I handed him his sandwich and a bottle of water.

"Damn, this the kind of treatment I get now? I could get used to this shit."

"So where have you been? Are you cheating on me already?" I said jokingly.

He looked at the ceiling saying only three words.

"Here we go."

I finally got my phone back so I could call my parents. Luckily I didn't have to do much convincing. I called my dad's cell phone. One thing I knew for sure was that Larry Brooks always picked up on the first ring. This time I didn't even hear it ring once.

"Baby, are you okay? Where are you? What's going on?"

"Calm down Daddy, I'm okay."

"Jesus Christ, we've been worried sick about you! I saw you on the news getting into the car with that man at the gas station. Who was that?"

I had no idea they knew about the shooting at the store or that it was even on the news already. "He's just a friend, Daddy. I really didn't wanna shoot that man but I had to, he could've killed us!"

"I understand that baby girl. You had to do what you had to do, but I think you should come home now. The police are looking for you, Angel. What are you gonna do?"

"I don't know yet," I said.

There was a knock on our room door. Leo and I looked at each other. I tried to lower my voice as I rushed off the phone.

"Daddy, tell Mom and Fletcher I said hey. I gotta go, love you, bye."

I hung the phone up before he had a chance to reply. Leo grabbed his gun off the nightstand and went to the door.

"Who is it?"

10

LEO

"Yooo, it's June bruh."

I put my gun on my waistline and opened the door to let him in.

"Oh, my bad bruh I ain't mean to interrupt."

"Nah, you good fam, come on in. This is Angel, Angel this is June."

"Nice to meet you," June said.

Angel smiled and nodded her head.

"Yo, my people need two zones big bruh. We can take it to 'em if you want."

I was excited at the chance to start making some money, I also wanted to see how much I could trust June. But I didn't want Angel to be alone right now.

"We were actually about to go grab a few things."

I tossed him two ounces.

"Be safe fam, we'll meet you back here later on."

"Sayless," he said.

We pulled out the motel parking lot headed to Wally World. I needed underclothes, toiletries, and sandwich bags. If I knew anything about females I was sure she needed some things as well. “Your Dad sounds like he’s worried about you.”

“Yeah, he is. He saw us on the news getting into my car at the gas station. He asked me who you were.”

“Yea, I heard you. So I’m just a friend, huh?”

She looked at me and smiled before biting her bottom lip.

“What about your mom?”

“I'm sure she’s worried too but not as much as my dad. We’ve always been like that; daddy’s girl-momma's boy. I have a little brother named Fletcher, he's nine.”

“Damn, that’s dope.”

“What’s dope?”

“Having a family, it sounds cool.”

“You don’t have a family?”

“Not really. It was just me and my parents until my mother was killed when I was seventeen, and my dad got arrested for her murder. He’s still in jail awaiting trial.”

“What! Oh my God.”

“I know it sounds bad, but he didn't do it though. My father’s not that type of person. Her real killer is out there somewhere and I have to find out who it is before it's too late. His trial date is coming up in a few months and I can't let him rot in jail for something he didn't do. Ever since I lost both of them I've pretty much been on my own.”

“Wow, that’s crazy.”

“Look, I don't want it to seem like I'm holding you hostage or anything.”

"You didn't say that when you had that gun to my ribcage!"

She was so full of jokes but so tough at the same time. I never met anybody like her. "You know what I mean, maybe you'll be safer with your family."

She unbuckled her seatbelt, flipped her body over onto the armrest, and laid the back of her head on my lap. Her beautiful brown eyes looked up at me as I drove.

"I don't wanna go back, I wanna stay with you."

She sounded like a little kid that didn't wanna go to school. I tried not to smile but I loved it. I loved the way she stared into my eyes. I loved the way she was submissive but still could hold her own when it came down to it. I loved everything about her. I couldn't tell her that though, it was too soon. Plus, I didn't want her to think I was soft and mushy. I had to make sure she knew I was none of that. But there was something about Angel, and I couldn't ignore the way I felt.

11

LEO

We moved swiftly through the aisles. Nobody knew exactly how much shit they needed until they went to Wal-Mart. Items rained into the buggy, which sounded like it needed a wheel alignment. I didn't like to go to Wal-Mart in Augusta because when I did I would always run into somebody I knew, asking questions about my father just being nosy. I didn't have to worry about that here. We were in a big city where the Black population helped us to blend in, but we still needed to move fast and smart. We couldn't be in here taking our precious time looking at posters and smelling different hygiene products. We hurried up and got what we needed. We would've done great on the old TV game show Supermarket Sweep.

Back at the motel, June was standing on the balcony as we pulled in.

"I'm glad you out here fam, you can help us take these bags up," I said jokingly. "Sayless, I got you bruh."

After helping us with the bags, June and I walked to his room to get squared away. I was questioning whether he would come back with the money. Two ounces is enough to make anybody run off, especially if they just met the person they got it from. Luckily he was looking at the bigger picture, which was more money to be made in the future. I got my money and he got his cut off the top. Too smooth, like the ocean up under the moon.

"My people said somebody named Sambo got lit up around the corner last night. Word on the street it was these twins, Travis and Tony. I wouldn't doubt it either. Them boys been round here wildin' out on some ruthless shit."

"What do you mean?" I asked.

"They move weight, but they're always getting into it with somebody. They came up here from Florida about a year ago, tryna take shit over. I guess some niggas just wasn't feeling it."

I nodded my head, taking in everything he was saying.

"Anyways, twelve probably gonna be extra hot around here for a while so be safe, bruh."

"Fasho," I said. "Always."

"Aye, you heard that?" June asked with a serious look on his face.

We stood quiet and looked at each other for a few seconds. There it was again... a woman's voice screaming from outside.

12

LEO

June and I rushed out the door onto the balcony. We peered over the rail to see who was causing all the commotion. To my relief, it wasn't Angel, but a short, slim, brown skinned chick with short hair. She looked like Nia Long's character Debbie, in the movie *Friday*.

"Gimme my fuckin money, Kevin!"

She was arguing with a heavy set light skinned guy with dreads.

"I ain't got yo money you stupid bitch!"

"I know you got it wit yo sorry ass, you the only one that had keys to my shop!"

When we reached the bottom of the steps we started inching closer to the domestic disturbance. A lot of the motel guests had also come out their doors to see what was going on. Even Angel was now gazing down from the second floor eating a Slim Jim as if she was watching a movie. "You probably spent it on drugs you fuckin junkie," she said.

That must've rubbed him the wrong way because, after a brief pause, the back of Kevin's hand came down on her face sending her straight to the ground. I looked over at June who was already looking at me. Reading each other's minds, an already shirtless June started walking toward fatso as I removed my shirt as well. We were both strong and dark so we kind of looked like Booker T. and Stevie Ray of the Harlem Heat. Kevin the woman beater was about to find himself in the middle of a Royal Rumble.

I hit him with the first blow which made him stumble a little but he managed to stay on his feet. June followed right behind me with combos of fury. I could tell he had been in quite a few fights by the way he swung his punches. The big fella didn't stand a chance. By the time we were finished with him, he was lying on the ground trying to catch his breath and spitting out blood. I sat him up on his butt and knelt behind him with my right arm around his neck. His arms hung by his side. He didn't have enough energy to fight back anymore.

"How much did he steal from you?" I asked.

"About a G," she said.

I looked at June and gave him a head nod towards Kevin's pockets. June wasn't a slow leak. It felt like we had telepathy or were separated at birth. June went in his pockets only to come out with a cell phone with a cracked screen and an almost empty box of Newports.

"He probably smoked it all up," she said.

My grip tightened around his neck. I glanced around at the onlookers and everything started to get quiet for a few moments. I felt a sense of power. It wasn't the same power as Scarface but it was still power. In a way, it felt good to have everybody watching as I took control of the situation. Even the group of kids had stopped playing to get a glimpse of the action. But there was too much attention on us. There were way too many eyes, and we didn't need any extra heat so I had to stop the show. I pushed him away from me and he just laid there on the pavement hardly able to move.

We headed back toward the stairway, and I signaled with my head for the short haired girl to follow us, which she did.

"Hey I'm Naudia," she said to Angel who was sitting on the bed as we walked in the room. "I'm Angel. I saw what happened to you. Are you okay?"

"Yea I'm good thanks, he hit like a bitch."

Everyone in the room laughed.

"So who was that?" I asked.

"My sorry ass ex-boyfriend, we broke up a few months ago. I knew he still had a key to my beauty shop. I should've got the locks changed but I never did, big mistake."

I reached in my pocket and counted out a thousand dollars in hundreds. I extended my hand to give it to her. "Forget about him."

Her eyes opened wide and she hesitated before slowly grabbing the money.

"Thank you so much, but why are y'all helping me?"

"Have you ever been to jail before?" I asked.

"No."

"So your record is clean?"

"Yeah, why?" she asked with a puzzled look.

"Let's just say we might be able to help each other," I replied. "Plus, I hate women beaters."

13

ANGEL

Leo and I sat in our room smoking and watching Seinfeld. I stared at him as he laughed hysterically.

"How can somebody as tough as you, laugh so hard at a show like this?"

"I don't care what nobody says, this shit is funny."

"I guess so," I said as I plopped down on his lap sideways and put one arm around his neck. "You got a mean right hook," I said as I looked into his eyes.

"You think so?"

"I know so, it made me wet a little bit."

He grabbed a handful of my ass and bit his bottom lip. My lady friend started to throb.

"Gimme dat tongue," he said.

My body tingled when he said that.

After having sex for about an hour I rested my head on his muscular chest. Keith Sweat and the Sweat Hotel played quietly on the motel radio. After beating up Naudia's ex-boyfriend earlier and then beating up my lady friend, I know Leo felt like the heavyweight champion of the world. He ran his fingers through my hair.

"What are you thinking about?" he asked.

I started to lie and tell him I was thinking about our future wedding ceremony, but I knew that would never happen so I told him the truth.

"My family, I know they miss me."

"Maybe you should go visit them, so they won't be worried about you. Why don't you go tomorrow? I'll just ride with June to handle that business with Naudia, you know we can't live in this motel for too long."

I rubbed his cheek.

"Yea, I know baby. Whatever you wanna do, I'm with you I promise."

He kissed me on my forehead. "Thanks, bae."

The drive to Augusta didn't seem too long since I was listening to a bunch of interviews and podcasts on YouTube almost the whole way there. When I was getting close I turned off YouTube and turned to 97.9 The Wiz. They were playing *Always Be My Baby* by Mariah Carey so I turned the volume up and sang at the top of my lungs.

When I pulled into my parent's quarter-mile driveway, I could smell the freshly cut grass of the fields on both sides. By the time I got to the house, my dad was racing out the door. "Baby Girl!"

"Hey, Daddy!"

I sunk into his arms for a long hug.

"I missed you so much, are you okay?"

"I'm fine Daddy."

"Some detectives came by here looking for you. They said they want to ask you some questions."

I rolled my eyes and let out a long breath."What's there to ask, the robber had us at gunpoint. The store clerk saw the whole thing."

"I don't know sweetheart, they probably just want to get a statement or something. Come on in, you hungry?"

I smiled, I was starving.

"Mom, can you pass the biscuits?" Fletcher asked.

She handed him the biscuits without taking her eyes off of me. Just like every woman, my mother had a strong intuition. She knew I was up to no good, and I couldn't look her in the eyes for too long. I looked down at my plate and started back eating.

"Who's that guy you were with on the news, sis?"

I stopped chewing and cut my eyes at him.

"He's just my friend."

"So did you tell him?" My mom asked.

Everything was awkwardly quiet for a few moments until my dad coughed.

"You know sweetheart, you should think about coming back to live with us," he said.

"Yeah sis, then I could have somebody to play Mortal Kombat with."

I turned to Fletcher and put my hand on his shoulder. "How about we play after dinner?"

His eyes lit up like the sky on the fourth of July.

"Really?"

"Of course, I'll even let you pick your player first."

"Okay deal!" he said smiling and continuing to eat.

When I got in my car to leave it felt like a weight had been lifted off my shoulders. Seeing my family was exactly what I needed. I stopped at the Circle K right beside Interstate Twenty to fill my gas tank before heading back to Atlanta. As I finished pumping gas, two middle-aged white men wearing suits approached me. One of them had a bald head. The other wasn't too far behind with only a few strands left which were combed over to the side.

"Angel Brooks, just the woman we've been looking for," said the bald one with a half smile on his face.

"Well you found me, so what the fuck do you want?"

"Easy there young lady. I wouldn't think that somebody who just shot and killed a man would be talking to law enforcement in that tone of voice."

He took off his shades and winked one of his eyes as if he had me exactly where he wanted. He was definitely giving crooked cop vibes.

"Anyways, it's not what we want, it's *who* we want."

His partner with a few strands of hair let out a small chuckle, other than that he was just standing there looking like Mr. Baldies' sidekick.

"We know Leo Bryant was with you when you shot that man at the store. We're certain you know his whereabouts. So why don't you be a smart woman and tell us where he is? Unless of course, you want to be charged with manslaughter, which could put you in prison for the next ten years, if you're lucky. You wouldn't want that now would you, Ms. Brooks?"

He extended his hand to give me a business card. Looking him in the eyes, I snatched it out of his hand.

"You got forty-eight hours young lady or you can expect an arrest warrant with your name on it. You have a nice day now."

They slowly turned around and walked back to their black SUV. I stood there trying to take in everything he just said. I also wanted them to leave before I did, so they wouldn't see which way I was going. Something about both of them gave me the creeps. I looked down at the business card Mr. Baldy gave me.

Lieutenant James T. Nelson

14

LEO

It was almost one o'clock in the afternoon and the sun was procrastinating its full potential in Thompson, Georgia. The GPS brought me to a slim dirt road with little space for two cars to pass each other. June let me borrow his black minivan without asking any questions about where I was going. I'm sure if I told him what I was doing, it wouldn't have mattered. Angel was visiting her family in Augusta and I had a few hours to do some investigating before I had to go look at a few houses with Naudia. I knew it wouldn't be long before we started drawing attention to ourselves from moving work out of the motel. We needed some low key spots, and for that, Naudia was our most valuable player.

It was a shot in the dark, but so was every other failed attempt to find my mother's killer. Frank Moore was convicted in 1996 of attempted murder by strangulation. From the story I read online, the victim's roommate came home while Moore was strangling her with an extension cord. The same way my mother was killed. It wasn't the only strangulation case I had found close to the Augusta area, but in all the other cases the suspects were still in prison. Moore had received a 20 year sentence for the attempted murder and had done eighty-five percent of his time. He was released about eight months prior to my mother's murder. Maybe it was a coincidence, maybe not.

I pulled into the dirt driveway of a small brick house. The yard was also dirt with patches of grass here and there. To the left of the house sat a shed that was bigger than the house. It had two open garage doors and inside was a radio playing *A Change Is Gonna Come* by Sam Cooke. As I walked up, I eased to the left a little bit so I could better see inside the shed. Before I could see all the way inside, a lady with brown skin and curly black hair walked out holding a butcher's knife. She wore a pair of dengue blue jeans and a dirty white t-shirt.

"Well hello there. Are you looking for someone?" she asked with a strong Southern accent and an inviting smile. "You look like you saw a ghost."

She looked down at the knife dangling in her hand below her waist and then looked back up at me.

"Oh I'm sorry, did I scare you? I was just cutting up some watermelon. You lost or sumthin'?"

"No mam I don't think so, I'm looking for Frank Moore."

She smiled and started laughing as she seemed to be looking for something in the sky. "Frank? Well, I'm sorry to tell you sugar, Frank has been gone for almost a year now."

I stood there realizing I probably should've done a little more homework before I rushed into this.

"Were you a friend of my husbands?" she asked.

"No mam," I said before looking down and then back up at her. "I'm trying to find out who killed my mother."

Her smile disappeared and her head dropped toward the ground. She nodded her head once and started walking toward the house.

"Come inside," she said.

Inside the house smelled of lavender. The kitchen had bright yellow walls. Putting two glasses on the counter, she filled both of them with lemonade and handed me one without asking if I was thirsty. "Thank you," I said as I took a small sip.

With her right leg crossed over her left leg, she stared at the floor as she began talking. "Frank fought that damn cancer for a long time. Even before I met him, but it finally got the best of him. I'm thankful we got to spend a few years together before it took him."

I watched her stare at a picture on the wall of the both of them as she seemed to be daydreaming of their memories together. When she realized what she was doing she snapped out of it and focused her attention back to me.

"So, what was your mother's name?"

"Her name was Linda, Linda Bryant. She was murdered over four years ago. Not even a year after your husband was released from prison. She was strangled."

The way silence filled the room I could tell she now understood exactly why I suspected her husband.

"I see," she said as she broke eye contact with me and took a sip of her lemonade. "Your mother was killed in the same way Frank did that girl that landed him in prison over twenty years ago. Is that what brings you here?"

"That's exactly what brought me here. Look, mam, I'm not accusing your husband of anything. I'm just looking for answers, that's all. I owe at least that to my mother."

"I understand young man, I really do. I can honestly tell you that while Frank was alive and free, he wasn't the same man he was twenty years ago. He was a loving and caring man. We went to church every Sunday. I hate he was in that rotten prison for so long, but that's where he found God. Even back then he would call me and we would pray on the phone together. When they finally did release him, I can't remember a day we didn't spend together. Now, I can't say with one hundred percent certainty what my husband did or didn't do because then I'd be lying. However, I will say this. I think your mother deserves justice and I hope she gets it, I really do, but honestly, I think you came to the wrong place."

I don't know if it was what she said or how she said it, but I believed her and started to realize she was probably right.

"You're probably right mam, I'm sorry for wasting your time." I stood up to leave. "Thanks for the lemonade."

"Wait a minute. Before you go, when exactly did it happen?"

I told her the exact date she was murdered, and that it happened sometime in the early morning. She thought about it for a few moments.

"I'm sorry, I can't remember that day off the top of my head. I wish I could be of more help."

"It's alright mam, you helped all you could. I appreciate it."

Before I left I gave her my number just in case she remembered anything. She gave me a watermelon she grew in the field behind her house. Watermelon was my mother's favorite fruit. When I told her that, she hugged me and wished me luck on my search.

15

LEO

Later that day after I brought back June's car, we sat patiently right behind Naudia's convertible Chrysler Sebring. She was around the corner viewing a four bedroom house. We needed a safe place to live without having to worry about the police kicking the door in. If everything worked out, next we were going to look at a smaller house. That would be headquarters. A spot that we could come back and forth to and move work out of.

"If all this goes through I think you should still keep the motel room for a while fam, just so nobody notices any changes. This way we can also keep an ear to the streets, you feel me?"

"Say less bruh," he said. "I like the way you think."

A few moments later Naudia came turning the corner smiling and handed me a set of keys. Things were going exactly as planned. I told her I would pay her rent at the beauty shop every month as long as she continued to keep the spots in her name. She was more than happy, and so was everybody else. It was time to level up.

I sat in the motel room counting money and smoking. Angel unlocked the door and came in. I had been waiting for her to get back so I could tell her the good news about our new spots. I dangled the keys in the air. "We're moving on up like George and Weezy!"

Her face had no expression. I knew something wasn't right.

"What's wrong?" I asked. "Why do you look like you saw a ghost? Are your people good?" "Yea they good, but these two bald head ass cops ran up on me at the gas station in Augusta." My heart skipped two beats as I rose to my feet.

"Man, get the fuck outa here."

"I'm serious, they said if I don't give you up in forty-eight hours they would charge me with manslaughter and put a warrant out for my arrest."

"What! Nah, don't worry, I'll turn myself in tomorrow. I can't let you go down for my bullshit. We can put things on hold for a while, and then when I get out—"

"No," she interrupted. "They can't charge me with that. It was self-defense. They're probably just trying to scare me into giving you up. I think they're bluffing. Don't worry about it, keep things going how they are. Fuck them. Let's get it."

My face lit up. I loved the little bit of thug she had in

her. I was glad she said that because I really didn't want to turn myself in.

"Okay," I said. "Fuck 'em, let's get it."

16

LEO

It was a busy day at Splash in the Boro in Statesboro, Georgia. The wave pool was packed. June and I lounged back in one of the many cabanas which were lined up on both sides. The sun shined brightly, stopping just outside of our cabana. The smell of chlorine, suntan lotion, and food danced through the waterpark. Angel and Naudia had gone to get on a waterslide that was right behind the back of our cabana. I laid back in my chair and let out a huge breath as I looked out at the artificial waves. It had been a while since I felt this calm.

My mother used to bring me here when I was a kid. I could still picture her rubbing suntan lotion onto her dark brown skin. She would clap and cheer me on as I jumped over each wave one after another. This was as close to peace of mind I could ask for right now. I deserved it. We all deserved it. I didn't exactly have the mansion and tiger like Scarface, but I had more money than I'd ever had. That made me feel good.

Things were going pretty smooth considering the circumstances of how I ended up here. Angel was driving back and forth to Augusta to get the work from Joe because it was a lot safer than me going. She could also stop and see her family whenever she wanted to. It had been over two months since she'd seen those cops and there still was no arrest warrant. It looked like she called their bluff. June had his people buying a lot more weight. He was becoming one of the heavy hitters on the east side. Like me, he moved smart and worked hard. To say that he was eating good was an understatement.

Naudia's beauty salon was doing great. I kept up the salon rent as agreed. I also gave her money on the side to show my appreciation for keeping everything in her name. Without her, we definitely wouldn't have been able to expand. Things were looking up for the four of us. Not only were we business partners, but we had become friends as well. Friends with money, and a lot of it.

I noticed a little chubby boy walking with his mom. He reached and grabbed a piece of pizza off of a table that another family had left behind. His mother yanked his arm and smacked the pizza out of his hand causing June and I to look at each other and bust out laughing.

Angel and Naudia walked back into the cabana with four chocolate milkshakes with whipped cream. My eyes twinkled. I loved chocolate.

"What yall laughing about?" Angel asked.

I looked over at June who was still smiling.

"You had to be here," I said.

I held my milkshake in the air.

"To the good life."

Everybody touched their shakes, smiled, and repeated.

"To the good life."

17

ANGEL

I drove Naudia's car and she rode shotgun as we sang along to *Why I Love You So Much* by my favorite singer and nineties R&B star Monica. I had never driven a convertible before. I felt like a celebrity as my hair blew in the wind. We pulled up to a gas pump. In front of our car, two men stepped out of a black impala with black rims and tinted windows. The first thing I noticed was their gold teeth gleaming in the sunlight. The driver wore wicks on top of his head and the passenger had dreads. Besides their difference in hairstyles, they looked exactly alike. They walked towards us. "How y'all beautiful ladies doing today?" the driver asked.

"We're good, but why y'all walking up on us like that?" Naudia shot back.

The driver put his hands up as if to let us know he didn't want any trouble.

"My bad lil mama, we just saw two beautiful ladies so we came to speak, no harm intended. My name is Tony and this is my brother Travis."

Travis took that as his cue to chime in.

"Y'all smoke? Y'all tryna come kick it with us for a little bit? We won't keep y'all long."

His proposal made me laugh.

"We don't even know y'all like that," I said. "Besides, y'all look like double trouble."

They both giggled, making sure all of their gold teeth were showing.

"Looks can be deceiving," Tony said. "And we can get to know each other, I'll even fill ya gas tank up."

He pulled out a hundred dollar bill and held it in front of me. I stared at it for a few seconds before taking it out of his hand.

"Well, I guess we do have a lil time to kill," I said looking over at Naudia.

She smiled.

"Yea, I guess so."

We followed the twins to a neighborhood in the suburbs. Every single house had a garage, and most of the houses were two stories. I took mental notes of every single turn we made. When we got to their house we exited our vehicles and followed them toward the back door.

"Oh shit, y'all ain't tell me y'all had a pool. I would've brought my bathing suit," I said.

"Or we could just go skinny dipping," Travis suggested.

"Uhhh, no thank you."

Tony shook his head at his twin brother as he opened the back door.

"Come on in, make yourselves at home, mi casa su casa," he said as he led us down a hallway and into the living room.

Naudia plopped down on the couch like she was at home.

"Dang, how yall get this big ass house and all this nice furniture? Wait lemme guess, y'all some rappers, huh?" she asked.

They laughed.

"Yeah, we rappers lil mama. I'd say we wrap 'em up pretty good," Tony said smiling as he busted down a cigar. "Yall want something to drink?"

"No thank you," Naudia said.

"Yeah I'm good too, but I do need to use your bathroom real quick."

Tony pointed toward the hallway. "Last door on the left, baby girl."

I grabbed my phone and purse and headed down the hall.

While heading to the bathroom, I could hear Travis talking to Naudia.

"Damn you got some lil ass feet girl, I might be able to put yo whole foot in my mouth."

That wouldn't be a bad idea, maybe then he would shut the fuck up.

18

LEO

After parking the car up the road, June and I laid low in a wooded area behind the twin's house. It didn't take long for the text that we were waiting for to come through.

Back door open.

We walked calmly through the backyard like we were supposed to be there. We crept through the back door of the house as slowly and quietly as possible. Laughter was coming from the other end of the hallway. It wasn't until that moment the full understanding of what we were about to do weighed on my mind. Even if I wanted to turn back it was too late now. I quickly erased those thoughts from my head. With carefulness and precision, we crept toward the voices with our masks on and guns out until we were close enough to hear their conversation.

"I hope yo friend not back there stinking up the bathroom," one of the twins said.

I gave June a head nod and we both turned the corner into the living room.

"The only thing that's gonna be stinking is you," I said.

Before they had any time to react, we fired multiple rounds in both of their chests. Their stunned bodies dropped to the floor as they lay there motionless. We took our masks off as Naudia got up and walked over to us. Angel came from around the corner. We all stood next to each other looking down at the lives we had just taken.

"I told them we had time to kill," Angel said.

Back at headquarters, we split up about one hundred thousand dollars in cash between the four of us. We didn't want to rob and kill the twins but we had to. They had gotten word that June and I had taken some of their clientele and were bragging about what they were gonna do when they saw us. They were planning on taking us out, so it was kill or be killed. The money was just a bonus. We were already straight financially, but this put us up even more. We all knew exactly what we had done, and amongst each other, we weren't ashamed of it.

We were on top of the world. Just like in the movies violins played in my head and everything was in slow motion as everybody smiled and laughed together holding their cuts of the money. I focused on Angel as she spread her money out and fanned herself with it as if she was at church. She was nothing short of her name. The only thing she was missing was the wings and a ray of light shining from her sides. Her smile was genuine and she had a deep appreciation for life. She saved mine more than once and for that, I owed her the world. I would always have her back. June held his cut of the money in one hand, with his other hand he peeled back the stack of money and released it a little bit at a time under his nose while he breathed in deeply and smiled. He was a soldier like me, strong, tough, smart, and most importantly loyal. He definitely leveled up. Opportunity came knockin' and he answered the door gratefully. Now look at him, cheesing from car to car. Naudia was the last piece to the puzzle. She fell in at the right time and place. She was a hustler at heart. She built her beauty shop from the ground up on her own. With all the gossiping that goes on in those places, she managed to keep everything on the hush about our operation. She smiled and held two stacks of money to her ears as if they were phones. She was more than happy to level up on the crime side.

It's crazy how in a few months I went from the police kicking in my door, to building an empire with strangers. We never intended to be a team, but we were. Four loners who became so close in so little time. Funny how life works.

19

LEO

Although things were going good, I knew there were only so many sunny days until the rain came down. We sold drugs, laundered money, and killed people, all while I was still on the run in Augusta. We were playing a very dangerous game. If every move wasn't calculated we could all end up in a cell for the rest of our lives. The thought alone made my stomach do backflips. It also made me think of my pops. I had to be smart. I had to beat the odds like Scarface. Most importantly, I still had to find out who killed my mother.

The four of us sat in the back corner of Tad's Steak House. The booths had tall seats that shielded us from the rest of the restaurant. Our waiter was a young white girl wearing all black. We stopped talking for a second while she came over and picked up some of our dirty plates.

"Did you guys save room for dessert? she asked.

Everybody started shaking their heads to decline.

"I think we're good," I said.

She came right back with the check and I picked up the bill. After all, it was my idea we came to eat in the first place.

I felt a sense of relief. During dinner, we discussed precautions that needed to be taken in order to keep business thriving. I explained that everybody needed to hide some money separately in a place where nobody would find it. If anybody was to go to jail for any reason, they were to obviously keep their mouths shut and also have no interaction with the others until they were released. Everybody agreed. I'm pretty sure we all thought alike, but now I was certain that we were all on the same page. Leaving the restaurant I felt good about our discussion. The next day we were to immediately start hiding money and tightening up on any loose ends that we could. We piled into Naudia's car to go home. Angel got in the passenger seat while June and I hopped in the back. There was a lightning strike in the sky so she closed the convertible top. We left the restaurant and pulled onto the interstate. Atlanta traffic was something that each of us hated. Nobody ever wanted to drive.

We were on the interstate for about twenty seconds before flashing blue lights appeared behind us out of nowhere.

"Oh shit," June said.

"Everybody stay calm, we're good," I said, not even believing it myself.

Naudia pulled over to the side of the road. We didn't even have a chance to come up with a game plan before he was approaching the passenger's side. Angel rolled down her window and he shined his flashlight on each of us, one after another.

"Good evening, my name is Officer Barnes with the DeKalb County Sheriff's Department. Do you know why I pulled you over tonight, mam?" His southern accent was thick which worried me a little.

"No I don't officer, but I know I wasn't speeding," Naudia said in her most trustworthy voice.

"No, you weren't speeding but you failed to use your turn signal when you merged onto the interstate back there. Where y'all headed tonight?"

"I was on the way to drop off my coworkers. We just came from a conference dinner." Which wasn't a lie.

"Oh yea?" he asked. "Where yall working?"

"At Lenscrafters," she shot back quickly.

Well, that was a lie. Still, I was impressed at the way she kept her composure and thought quickly under pressure.

"You got your license and registration, mam?"

She reached in the glove compartment to grab her papers before handing them to him. He shined his flashlight on her license.

"Hmmm, y'all hang tight," he said before walking back to his patrol car.

20

LEO

June didn't waste any time.

"You think we should take this motherfucker outta here?"

He was ready for whatever. He was a soldier at heart and I loved the way he stayed on go, but my intuition told me not to move too fast.

"Nah just be cool fam, let it play out. If he tries to get us out of the car, then we gotta do what we gotta do.

"You think he knows something?" Naudia asked.

"I doubt it."

The next few minutes felt like an eternity. Everybody was quiet. The only thing you could hear was Angel blowing bubbles with her gum in the front seat. I swear nothing phased her. My mind was racing. This couldn't have come at a worse time. Right before we were supposed to put some money up. Was it really going down like this? *Lord just give me one more chance.* Situations like these had a way of making everybody religious all of a sudden.

There it was. The sound of the police cruiser door slamming shut. It sounded like the firing of a gun at an Olympic race or the ringing of a school bell right before a big fight. It was go time. “Here he comes,” Naudia said. I had my pistol in my hand as I prepared for the worst. I looked at June and he nodded his head to let me know we were on the same page. When the officer was back at our car he shined his flashlight on Naudia again.

“You said y’all worked at Lenscrafters, correct?”

“Yes sir.”

“Well mam, there's just one little problem with that,” he said.

Sweat started to form on my forehead. My grip tightened around my gun as I sat up a little bit to position myself for what was about to take place.

“Mam, if you sell glasses and whatnot, then how come you didn't *see* to it that you used your turn signal.” He chuckled at his own corny joke. He stopped laughing when he realized none of us found it funny. “Anyways I wrote you a warning. Make sure to always use your turn signal. Here's your information back. Y’all be safe now, ya hear.”

He tapped his hand twice on the roof of the car before walking off.

As soon as he shut the door on his cruiser we all laughed at the same time. What a relief, I could finally breathe normally again. I laid my head back on my seat, let out a long breath and looked at June.

“We gotta put that money up.”

21

LEO

After the traffic stop scare, we all moved a little bit smarter over the next few weeks. Business continued to grow and we each put money up as we agreed. I dropped the barbell on the rack to end my set of twenty as June stood behind me to spot. Our mini home gym consisted of a weight bench, pull up bar, dip bar, and some twenty-five pound dumbbells. We worked out every day to keep our muscles strong as well as our minds. We both pushed each other to go harder.

After our workout, we took showers, got dressed, and headed downtown to do a little light shopping. June had been doing most of the driving lately so we decided I would drive today. It was a beautiful Saturday. The mall parking lot was full of cars. Groups of people walked in and out the front doors as we rode around looking for a parking spot listening to *Leash On Life* by Starlito, Don Trip, and Kevin Gates. I finally saw someone backing out, so I put my turn signal on. Another car pulled up on our passenger side.

"I know damn well they ain't tryna steal our spot," I said.

The car's driver window rolled down and gunfire erupted. Glass shattered as bullets ripped through the passenger side of our car. There was no time to react. Gunshot after gunshot hit both me and June again and again until finally tires screeched as the gunman sped off. Panicked bystanders were screaming and running for cover. My body was locked up, unable to move. I managed to turn my head to look over at June, only to realize his eyes were closed and he wasn't moving at all. "Fuck," I said barely able to get the word out.

There was blood all over my body and I could start to taste the blood filling my mouth. I flexed my muscles and grit my teeth trying to fight for my life, although I felt like I couldn't fight for long. Somehow going to sleep seemed like it would be better than the physical pain and mental regret that pierced through my mind and body. I knew there was a good chance I could go out like this, but I didn't think it would be this soon. I wasn't ready to leave this world, not yet. My father needed me. I continued to flex as hard as I could, but I felt my body getting weaker and I was still unable to move. While trying to achieve the power and greatness of Scarface, I had forgotten one thing. He died in the end. If I died maybe I'd get to see my mother again. That alone was worth it. I thought of her smiling face and somehow everything seemed like it was going to be okay. I looked at June, he was still motionless. "Damn bruh," I said as I closed my eyes.

22

LEO

I woke up unsure of where I was. Still dazed, it took me a few seconds after I opened my eyes to realize I was handcuffed to a hospital bed. I could have woken up anywhere and still been grateful. At least I was alive. I had another chance at life. Then I remembered how June looked in the passenger seat. I tried to yell but struggled to get anything out. I banged on the side of the bed with my free hand until a nurse came rushing in.

"Mam!" I said as my body began to ache from yelling out.

An attractive brown skinned nurse rushed over to me.

"Sir, you need to calm down before you hurt yourself. Your body is under a lot of stress and it needs to relax. My name is Nurse Nichole by the way."

"The guy that was with me, is he okay?"

"He's alive but he's non-responsive. I'm sorry to tell you this but he's barely holding on. Both of you were shot multiple times, you four and him seven, including once in the head."

I sat back. He was still alive. We were both blessed to still be here.

"What's up with the handcuffs?" I asked, acting like I didn't know.

"You have some warrants out of Richmond County. As soon as you get healed up they'll be sending someone to transport you there. We have to restrain you until then."

She leaned in closer, "Just a heads up there's an officer in the hallway keeping watch."

I recognized her fragrance and it brought back a nostalgic feeling. Anytime a smell made me feel like that, I figured it was a perfume one of my elementary teachers used to wear.

"Thanks," I said as she headed to the door.

She kept walking out but threw two fingers up in a peace sign before turning the corner into the hallway. I looked down at the ugly baby blue hospital gown they had on me. I had no memory of putting it on. I wondered who might have seen me naked. Maybe that's why Nurse Nichole was being so nice to me.

Who the hell tried to kill us? I had no idea and I wasn't about to stress myself trying to figure it out. Maybe June would pull through with more answers. Maybe he saw something. Maybe it was somebody he was beefing with that I didn't know about. I tried resting my brain. I knew I had to go back to Augusta to face those charges. I might as well try to get some well needed rest. I thought about Angel and Naudia and what they might be doing as I drifted off to sleep.

. . .

I woke up to Nurse Nichole knocking on the door as she walked in.

"Wake up Leo, you have a visitor."

I breathed out a long, heavy breath and rolled my eyes because I told them not to have any communication with me if anything like this was to go down. To my surprise it wasn't Angel or Naudia who walked in behind Nichole, it was Joe.

He came in with confidence in his walk like he always did, chin up and chest out. His shirt was tucked in as usual. Joe cared about me so much he came to see me even if it meant risking his freedom. That's the type of person he was. Loyalty and principles were everything to him. "I'll leave you two alone," Nichole said as she strode out the door.

"Glad to see you still alive, kiddo. Not too many people can take that many bullets." He sat down a light blue envelope on the table next to my bed. I glanced over at it and read what it said out loud.

"Get well soon," I said. "I hope so, you know you didn't have to come see me."

"Yea I know, there's a lot of things I don't have to do. The question is, what kind of man would I be if I didn't do 'em."

Joe had a deep answer for everything, almost like a philosopher.

In the twenty minutes Joe was in the room with me we didn't say anything incriminating. We didn't speak on drugs, money, or mention anybody's name that was involved in my organization. What we did talk about was memories. We reminisced on the good times back in the day when I was just a kid and my mother was still alive. It brought me happiness to be able to share laughs with somebody about when times were a lot simpler. Joe was like family. Before he left he told me not to worry about anything when I got to the jail because he was gonna keep money on my books. I told him thank you, but I was more thankful for him than he would ever know.

In the four days that passed, Nichole and I had gotten pretty close. She played UNO with me, told me stories of her family, and even watched a little TV with me when she had some downtime. Most importantly she was helping me get my health back to normal. In that little time, I must've asked her about June's condition at least a dozen times. Each time it was the same thing, still unresponsive, but still alive. The latter was all I cared to hear.

I looked at the clock, it was time for Seinfeld. I grabbed the remote, but before I could change the channel Nurse Nichole was walking in. She didn't have her usual smile. I feared the worst thinking about June as she got closer to my bed.

"The Richmond County Sheriff's office is here to transport you."

I let out a sigh of relief.

"It's all good, thanks for taking care of me. I won't forget about you."

She smiled and put her hand on my shoulder.

"No problem Leo, I won't forget about you either. Just make sure you stay out of trouble." I smiled back at her.

"I got you."

Two Black bulky uniformed officers stepped in the door.

"Mr. Bryant, are you ready to go on vacation?"

It be your own people. I threw my head back on the bed and looked up at the ceiling. "Here we go."

In the car, the officers talked about everything from the Freak-Nik to the Hoover vacuum cleaner. I tried my best to ignore them. The empire we built was crumbling beneath my feet. Maybe with some twist of fate, June would pull through and he, Angel, and Naudia would continue to prosper. When I got out they would all be waiting on me outside the gates so we could all ride off into the sunset with the top down. In reality, it probably wouldn't go that smooth. What I was sure of, was that my stash spot was presidential. Eventually, I would get out of jail and go back for the money I had put up. I felt terrible about letting Angel down. I was supposed to be there for her, especially after all she had done for me. I tried to stay positive. Maybe it was a good thing for her. She could get back to her family now and live a good, safe life from here on out. That's what she deserved.

Barbed wire fences interrupted my thoughts. We slowed down and turned into the county jail. Dumbo number one let down the driver's window.

"One Bravo Mike"

23

LEO

It took just under a week for me to get classified, but I was finally getting moved into the general population. I was glad because sitting in that cell all day was getting old. I had already sent word to my father to let him know that I was here. I stood in the sally port looking through the glass into the open pod. Cubicles lined the pod walls on both sides. The dayroom was in the middle of the open pod with a high hanging television and tables. The chairs were stacked against the back plexiglass wall. On the other side of the plexiglass was a small rectangular rec yard with concrete walls. It didn't take long before I spotted my father. We stood there looking at each other like two fish in two separate bowls. Both of us wore a smile that could light up heaven. Since he's been locked up we've only had phone calls and video screen visits. The other times I went to jail, I either bonded right out, or they ended up putting me in a different pod. It had been almost five years since we'd seen each other in person. The guard took the handcuffs off me and I put my hands on the wall as he patted me down.

"Alright Bryant, you're good," he said.

The door to the pod popped open and I walked through. I dropped my things on the floor and opened my arms to embrace my father. He was the only family I had left and it felt good to have him back, even if we were in jail.

For two months we hung out together every day. We usually walked side by side doing laps around the small rec yard. All we had was time so I told him about everything that happened since that day I got off the phone with him and they kicked my door in. I also told him about all my failed attempts to find my mother's killer.

My father and I were also spades partners and would usually whoop anyone that sat down to play us, this day was no different. We were running the table on our opponents when the guard called my father's name. He heard him but that didn't stop him from slamming cards down on the table and talking shit to our opponents as I racked up every book. The guard shouted much louder this time. "Percy Bryant, pack your stuff you're going home!"

We looked at each other and I smiled in excitement but he squinted his eyes. Other inmates started to clap and cheer for him because of how long he had been there. What cards he had left in his hand fell to the table and he strode to the guard's desk.

. . .

After talking to the guard he made his way to his bunk and I damn near beat him there.

"I don't know what's going on son. They must've found the person responsible."

"I hope so," I said.

I helped him pack his five years worth of property into his net bag and plastic bin. He left me with a bunch of things he would no longer need now that he was going to be back in the free world. When we finished packing everything up, we hugged.

"I promise you, when I get out we gon be straight for life."

"I already know. Good luck in court, I love you, son."

"I love you too, Pops."

I watched as they took him out of the Sally port and down the hallway. Did they really find my mother's killer? My mind was racing with questions.

24

LEO

"Aye let me get next on the phone," I said as I walked past one of the dorm phones. He must've been in deep conversation because his head was down and all I got was a thumbs up. I paced back and forth anticipating the news I was about to hear about my mother's murder. Not only that, but I had also asked my father to reach out to Nurse Nichole to get an update on June. When it was my turn, I sat on the floor under the phone with my back against the wall. I had a feeling that whatever I was about to hear, I was gonna need to be sitting down. He pressed one before the operator could even finish the instructions. "Wassup Son."

"Wassup Pops, how you doing?"

"I'm good, Leo."

There was a pause before he continued talking.

"A fucking pig."

At first, I didn't register what he was trying to say. "Say what?" I asked.

. . .

"It was a crooked ass cop that killed your mother. I'm sorry you to have to hear it like this, son. He murdered Linda, another woman in Augusta, and one more in Aiken, SC.

"What the fuck!"

"Yea son, they said he wrote a confession letter before killing himself. I guess he didn't wanna take all that guilt with him to hell. What's crazy is, if he never wrote that letter, I'd probably be sitting in jail for the rest of my life for something I didn't even do."

I couldn't believe it. For almost five years I've searching for my mother's killer, and this whole time it was a fuckin' cop. I was looking in all the wrong places.

"His name was Lieutenant James T. Nelson," he said.

That was the same name that was on the business card. The one Angel had gotten from those cops who ran up on her at the gas station. That's probably why he wanted me in jail so bad because he knew I was looking for him. Sick fuckin bastard.

"Hey son, are you still there?"

"Yea, I'm here."

"Listen son, I just wanted to tell you, thanks for never doubting me."

"Come on now Pops, I know you would have never done that to Mom. I'm just glad you're free now, that's all I ever wanted."

"Yea me too, I've been in there so long I gotta get adjusted to the real world again. A lot has changed out here."

"I'm sure you'll be okay. Hey, did you ever get in touch with the nurse?"

"Yeah, I called up there. She told me they released him a few weeks ago and he was doing much better."

My cheeks rose and my head flew back as I exhaled a long breath of relief. My boy pulled through.

"I appreciate it, Pops."

"No problem, he even sent a message through the nurse. He said to tell you, *beauty shop bandit* whatever that means."

It was Kevin, Naudia's ex-boyfriend. He was the one who shot us. I should've known. Not too many people can take an ass whoopin' like that and not want revenge.

"You have two minutes remaining on this call."

"Look Pops, thanks again, I'm gonna keep in touch. Don't forget, when I get out it's on and poppin'."

"You just take care of yourself in there Leo, and let me know when you go to court so I can make sure I'm there."

"I got you."

"Alright boy, I love you."

"Love you too Pops."

25

LEO

After my workout, I decided to get in a few pages of Supreme Clientele by Ashley and JaQuavious. I had some time to kill before it was my turn in the shower anyway. Reading, working out, and sleeping were the best escapes of what I knew as my new reality. "Sorry to interrupt you, Leo." I looked up to see George, one of the older guys in the pod. He dumped almost half of a pillowcase of honeybuns on my bunk. He had run up a healthy bill from me loaning him snacks and hygiene products over the past few weeks. I didn't mind, especially because he was a friend of my father's. "I told you I was gonna pay you back now, didn't I?"

"Yeah you did G, I appreciate you."

"Nah, I appreciate you. You looked out for me when nobody else would. You got a good heart just like your dad, don't ever change that young blood." He gave me a fist bump before he walked to the other end of the pod.

It must've been my day. Earlier I had gotten a letter from my attorney saying we would be in court in a few weeks. That was great news since I didn't have a bond. They labeled me a flight risk since I ran when they raided my house. That meant I had to sit until my trial, which was soon thankfully. I was ready to get sentenced and go on up the road so I can get out of this petty ass jail and get my bid started, no matter how long it would be.

I headed towards the shower thinking about Angel. I missed her so much. Not a day went by that I didn't think about her. How we met, how fearless she was, how good she was in bed. In the shower, I thought about sliding in and out of her waterpark. I pleasured myself using just the right amount of soap and water. I aimed toward the drain on the shower floor as I finished. Thank God for shower shoes.

I was dozing off on my bunk when I heard the guard call my name. I slid into my shoes and headed towards his desk.

"The chaplain would like to see you," he said.

The strength in my legs disappeared and my body felt empty. Damn, not my Pops. Anytime someone got a visit from the Chaplain, it was to inform them of the death of a family member. I stood in the sally port feeling more alone than ever before. My Pops was the only real family I had left. I feared for the worst. Another officer stepped in, patted me down, put cuffs on me, and led me down the hall.

I sat in an empty room with nothing but a bunch of folded chairs stacked neatly against the wall. After a few minutes, the Chaplain walked in wearing a very well-tailored navy blue suit and was carrying a bible with a white envelope sticking out of it.

"How are you doing, young man?"

"I've been better but I'm okay."

"I understand that. I take it you know what I'm here to do."

Him saying that was all the confirmation that I needed.

"Yeah, I know, what happened to him?" I asked.

"Excuse me, sir," he said with his head tilted and eyes squinting.

"You came to tell me about my father right? What happened to him?"

"I'm sorry to inform you of this. Someone has passed, but it is not a he, it's a she." My eyes grew wide. The energy of my body switched to a different realm of fear. I stared into the soul of the Chaplain through his eyes waiting for him to tell me who *she* was.

"I'm sorry young man, but it's your friend Ms. Angel Brooks."

I let out a gasp as my head fell into my arms. Tears instantly filled my eyes. He put his hand on my shoulder.

"What happened to her?" I asked with my head still in my lap.

"She's been fighting cancer for quite some time now. Again, I'm terribly sorry. Nobody wants to hear anything like that, especially in a place like this. Normally we don't do this type of thing, but her father and I, Mr. Larry Brooks went way back. We used to play football together at Lucy C. Laney High School. Here you go, young man."

I lifted my head out of my lap to see him handing me the envelope with my name on the front. I took it out of his hand.

"I'll leave you alone for a while, just knock on the door when you're ready to go back." I nodded my head to acknowledge him as my eyes never left the envelope. The pain I felt was so bad I didn't feel like saying anything.

After he was gone, I held the envelope for a minute looking at it as I tried to take everything in. As soon as I opened the seal I could smell her wonderful distinctive fragrance. It was the same smell from the first time we met, when I kidnapped her and forced her into her jeep, the same smell as when we laid together laughing and talking about life. I couldn't believe she was really gone. How did I not see it? I pulled the paper out of the envelope and opened it up. Red and pink hearts descended down both sides of the paper. A single tear dropped from my eye and landed on one of the pink ones.

26

ANGEL

Leo,
If you're reading this that can only mean one thing, I'm gone. I've been battling with cancer for a while now. I'm so sorry I didn't tell you, but I had my reasons. The doctor predicted I had about one year to live. I wanted to spend the rest of the time I had left feeling alive. You helped me to do exactly that. During the time we spent together, I felt invincible, like nothing mattered. It felt like the world was ours. Remember our first time meeting at the grocery store, I was thinking, this motherfucker has no idea! Lol
There were a few times that I wanted to tell you but didn't, like when I was lying on your chest after our first time or when I was lying in your lap on the way to Wal-Mart. I knew you had a lot on your plate and I didn't want you to worry about me. I wanted you to see me as a regular person, not someone who was on their deathbed. But enough about me, you're a great person Leo. You're the sweetest, kindest, funniest, smartest, toughest, bravest, most loyal, and most handsome person I've ever met. Don't ever forget that. You will go on to

do great things. As far as I'm concerned you already have. Of course, I will be watching over you to make sure of it.

I love you so much, more than you'll ever know. I'll be sure to give your mother a hug for you and tell her how much you love and miss her.

Love Always, Your Guardian,

Angel

P.S. If and when you start to miss me or life seems to not be going your way, put on one of these songs and I will be right there with you, to help brighten up your day.

For You I Will by Monica

Angel Of Mine by Monica

I Will Always Love You by Whitney Houston

EPILOGUE

Me and five other guys walked out of the prison gates and onto a bus that would take us to a bus station and give us one free ticket to whatever city in Georgia we needed to go. The other five guys were talking loudly to one another, ecstatic about getting out. They talked about the things they were gonna do when they reached their destination. A couple of them talked excitedly about the first thing that they would eat. I was quiet. I looked out of the window taking in the realization that I was almost a free man again.

The Judge sentenced me to two years and I only ended up doing about twelve months. Six months into my bid I got caught with a couple pounds of tobacco and a few cell phones. They shipped me to another yard and took my canteen, visitation, and phone privileges away. Which caused me to slip into a state of depression. I did the last half of my bid not saying much to anybody. The bus came to a stop. The other five guys rose to their feet immediately and started making their way toward the front of the bus. I stayed seated until they were gone and then I got up and headed toward the exit. The bus driver gave me a strange look.

"What's the matter, you don't wanna go home?" he asked calmly.

I didn't say anything. I just looked at him and smiled before walking off the bus. I went to the booth to get my bus ticket for Augusta. While standing in line I felt a hand on my shoulder and turned around immediately. To my surprise, it was my father.

"I see you getting big, you must've been doing your pushups in there."

I dropped my bag and we hugged each other tighter than I can ever remember. It had been a while since we were both free. The feeling was like none other than I had felt in a long time. "I wasn't expecting you to be here, Pops. What are you driving?"

He smiled and pointed behind me. I turned around and across the parking lot, I saw June and Naudia leaning up against a bright red 1964 convertible Chevy Impala with twenty-inch spokes. The exact same car from the poster in his hotel room. They both were smiling and June threw both of his hands up in the air.

We walked over to them, June went to dap me up and it instantly turned into a hug. "Welcome home, my boy!"

"Preciate you fam!"

After hugging Naudia, something in the backseat of the car caught my eye. It was a car seat with a beautiful little baby girl.

"Who's baby?" I asked.

June and Naudia looked at each other, smiled, and then looked back at me.

"What!" I said with my fist over my mouth.

"That's crazy! Congratulations to y'all! What's her name?" I asked

They looked at each other once again before June looked back at me.

"Angel."

Tears started to form in my eyes as I reached over to baby Angel and started to tickle her stomach with my index finger. She smiled at me and giggled and my heart started to melt. June and Naudia got in the front. Me and Pops sat in the back with Angel.

"Any requests, bruh?" June asked as he turned on the tunes.

"Yea, play *For You I Will* by Monica"

"You got it, bruh."

We rode off into the sunset listening to the lovely voice of Monica. It felt like Angel herself was singing directly to me. It felt good to have my father back again. It also felt good to have the team back as well, June, Naudia, and of course, baby Angel.

Thank you to my son Luca for being my biggest inspiration. You're the reason I started writing. Daddy loves you so much.
Thank you to my mother Lori for standing behind me 100% in anything I do. Love you ma.
Thank you to my editor Bianca Shakur for your amazing work.
Thank you to all my family and friends who believe in me.

Made in the USA
Las Vegas, NV
15 September 2025

27941775R00066